Great Blue,
How Do You Do?

Written by Robin E. Kirk

Illustrated by Gail M. Nelson

"How Do You Do?"
Robin E. Kirk

Published and printed by:

Steuben Press

An Imprint of R&R Graphics, Inc.

8547 E. Arapahoe Rd., J240
Greenwood Village, CO 80112
303-339-0186

Printed in the United States of America

ISBN 978-1-935787-06-8

For Mrs. Betty Watson, with gratitude for sharing the wonder and delight found in children's literature.

For Ranger Beth, Ranger Meg, and Ranger Paul for listening and encouraging, thank you.

R.E.K

For my daughter, Katie, who is enthralled every time we see a Great Blue.

G.M.N

While on the train today
traveling through his national park,
Maestro heard about a great big bird
and this is what he learned.

Read about the Great Blue Heron
and as you do,
share some things about you, too.

Great Blue,

How Do You Do?

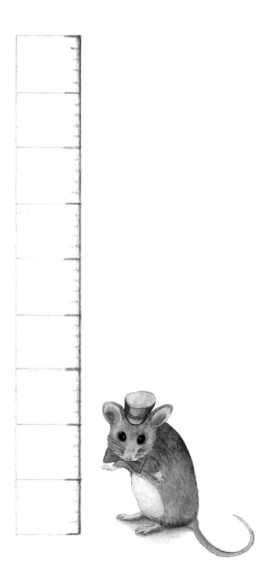

"I stand four feet tall, and you?"

Great Blue,
How Do You Do?

"I weigh a little more than pounds of four.

How much do you weigh
standing on the floor?"

Great Blue,

How Do You Do?

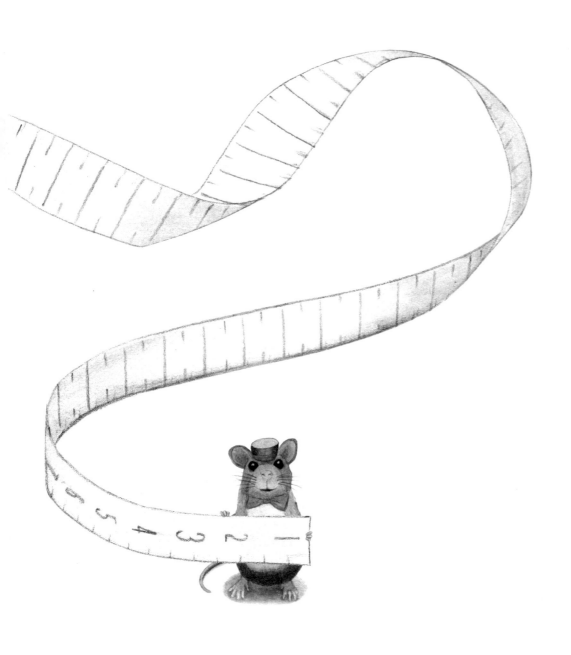

"When measuring my wingspan, it can be up to 7 feet."

Stretch out your arms and measure from fingertip to fingertip.

Great Blue,
How Do You Do?

"I live near wetlands
or along rivers.
You might see me high up
in the timbers.
My nest can be at rest
near saltwater or
water that is fresh."

Great Blue,

How Do You Do?

Heron nests are typically 30 to 70 feet high.

"My home is a large nest built with sticks, twigs, and reeds.
For my growing heron family
I have to please!

My nest can rest high in the sky in tall, tall trees that sway gently in the breeze, surrounded by water that catches the falling leaves."

Great Blue,

How Do You Do?

"I like to go fishing, do you?
I fish for my food, just to mention a few:
I eat frogs, insects, snakes,
and fish, of course, are a tasty treat.

What are your favorite foods
that you like to eat?"

Great Blue,
How Do You Do?

"Sometimes I travel to warmer climates
in the winter and sometimes
I stay where it is cold.

What weather do you enjoy –
warmer days
filled with the sun's rays
or hours of snow showers?"

Great Blue,
How Do You Do?

An embryo is an
unhatched chick.

"My eggs, numbering from two to six, sometimes seven, are rolled by each parent every few hours to keep them evenly heated so the developing embryo grows."

Great Blue,

How Do You Do?

Heronries are the nesting colonies for the Great Blue Herons.

Coming in late April or early May,
you can sense the excitement in the
heronries as the eggs begin to hatch
and the young herons
break through their shells.

It is a happy time, as you can tell.

Great Blue,
How Do You Do?

*Nestlings are
young herons
not yet ready to
leave the nest.*

May and June are busy months in the heronries. Mom and Dad are bringing food to the growing nestlings.

"Feed me! Feed me! Feed me," it seems the babies are saying, while the trees in the warm breezes are swaying.

Great Blue,

How Do You Do?

Fledglings are young birds with new flight feathers.

It's time.

Mom and Dad heron
have been successful in raising their young.

It's July and it's time to say *good-bye* to the fledglings.

They are ready to fly!

Maestro looks out his window from car #3 and watches the young Great Blue Heron. It's a thrill to see, and he wants to share it with you and me.